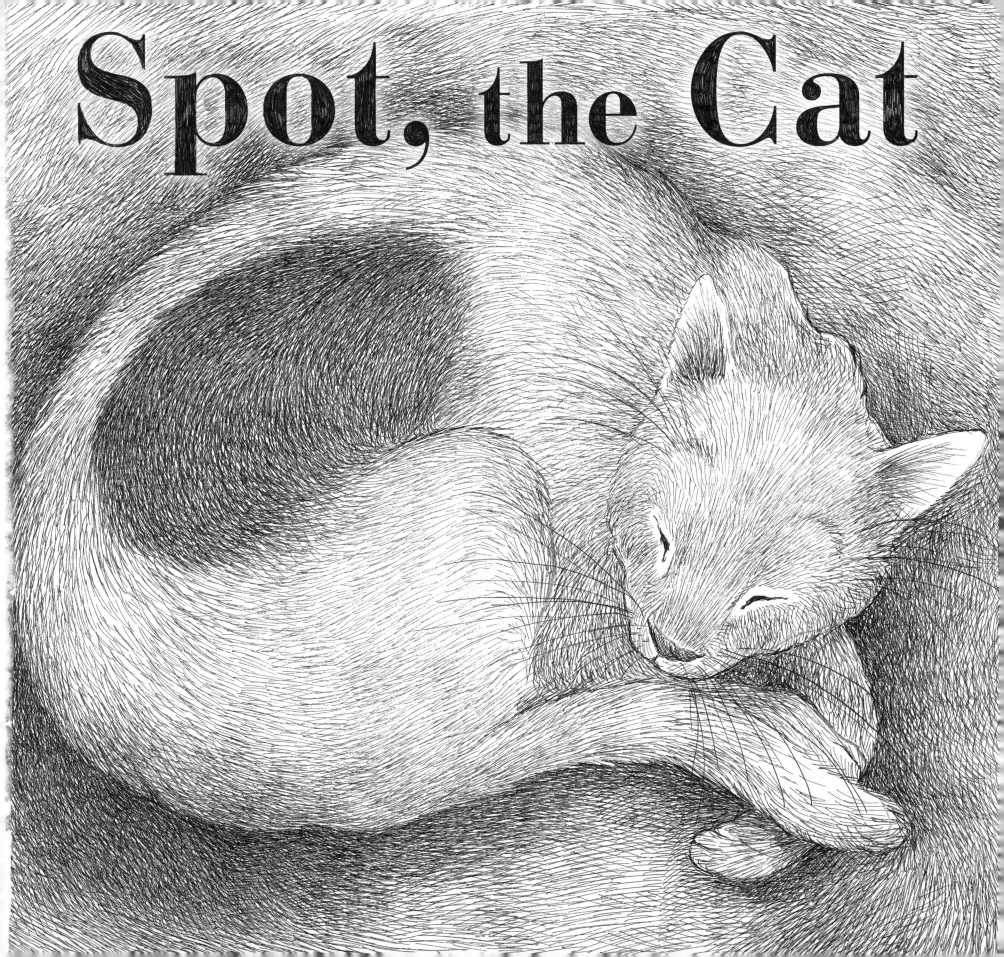

With much appreciation and affection,
to Laura and Hannah

LITTLE SIMON
An imprint of Simon & Schuster Children's Publishing Division
1230 Avenue of the Americas, New York, New York 10020
First Little Simon hardcover edition March 2016
Copyright © 2016 by Henry Cole
All rights reserved, including the right of reproduction in whole or in part in any form.
LITTLE SIMON is a registered trademark of Simon & Schuster, Inc.,
and associated colophon is a trademark of Simon & Schuster, Inc.
For information about special discounts for bulk purchases, please contact Simon & Schuster
Special Sales at 1-866-506-1949 or business@simonandschuster.com.
The Simon & Schuster Speakers Bureau can bring authors to your live event. For more
information or to book an event contact the Simon & Schuster Speakers Bureau at
1-866-248-3049 or visit our website at www.simonspeakers.com.
Designed by Laura Roode
Manufactured in China 1215 SCP
2 4 6 8 10 9 7 5 3 1
Library of Congress Cataloging-in-Publication Data
Cole, Henry, 1955– author, illustrator.
Spot, the cat / Henry Cole. — First Little Simon hardcover edition.
pages cm
Summary: In this wordless picture book, a cat named Spot ventures out an open window and
through a city on a journey, while his owner tries to find him.
ISBN 978-1-4814-4225-1 (hc : alk. paper) — ISBN 978-1-4814-4226-8 (eBook)
[1. Cats—Fiction. 2. City and town life—Fiction. 3. Lost and found possessions—Fiction.
4. Stories without words.] I. Title.
PZ7.C67345Br 2016
[E]—dc23
2015033267

Spot, the Cat

HENRY COLE

LITTLE SIMON

New York London Toronto Sydney New Delhi